A Beautiful Feast for a Big King Cat

A Beautiful Feast for a Big King Cat

by John Archambault and Bill Martin, Jr.

pictures by Bruce Degen

HarperCollins*Publishers*

A Beautiful Feast for a Big King Cat
Text copyright © 1989 by Silver, Burdett & Ginn Inc.
Illustrations copyright © 1994 by Bruce Degen
First published as part of the *World of Reading* basal reading series. This edition
published by special arrangement with Silver, Burdett & Ginn Inc.
Printed in the U.S.A. All rights reserved.

Library of Congress Cataloging-in-Publication Data
Archambault, John.
  A beautiful feast for a big king cat / by John Archambault and Bill
Martin, Jr. ; pictures by Bruce Degen.
      p.   cm.
  Summary: A little mouse who habitually teases a cat must use his wits
to avoid being eaten.
  ISBN 0-06-022903-9. — ISBN 0-06-022904-7 (lib. bdg.)
  [1. Mice—Fiction.   2. Cats—Fiction.   3. Stories in rhyme.]
I. Martin, Bill, date.   II. Degen, Bruce, ill.   III. Title.
PZ8.3.A584Be   1994   92-32331
[E]—dc20   CIP
                                                             AC

                1 2 3 4 5 6 7 8 9 10
                            ❖
                      New Edition

For Kevin Allen Archambault
—who teased his big brother Arie and ran, ran, ran
J.A.

For the Gibsons,
thanks for the real feast
B.D.

*"Big cat, big cat,
catch me if you can!"*
The mouse teased the cat
and ran, ran, ran.

He ran through the meadow
and ran through the wood,
all the way home
as fast as he could.

"Mother, O Mother,
please, save me from the cat!
He is bigger than big
and fatter than fat!"

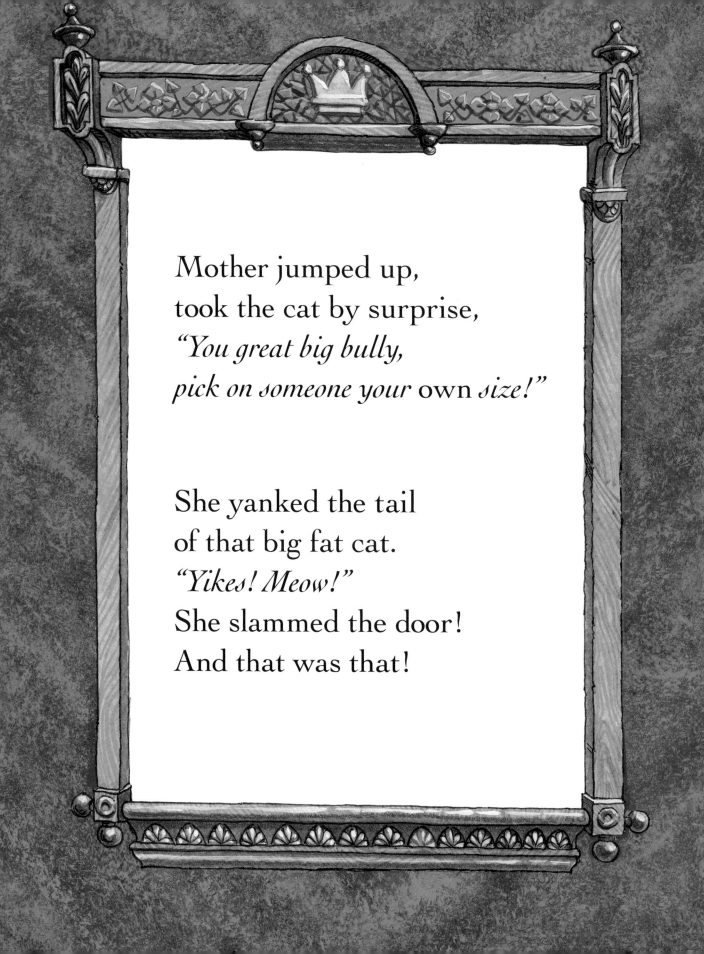

Mother jumped up,
took the cat by surprise,
*"You great big bully,
pick on someone your* own *size!"*

She yanked the tail
of that big fat cat.
"Yikes! Meow!"
She slammed the door!
And that was that!

*"Big cat, big cat,
catch me if you can!"*
The mouse teased the cat
and ran, ran, ran.

He ran through the meadow
and ran through the wood,
all the way home
as fast as he could.

"Mother, O Mother,
quick, open the door!
The big fat cat
is here once more!"

Mother jumped up
with fire in her eyes,
"You great big bully,
pick on someone your own *size!"*

She tweaked the nose
of that big fat cat.
"Yikes! Meow!"
She slammed the door!
And that was that!

"*Big cat, big cat,*
catch me if you can!"
The mouse teased the cat
and ran, ran, ran.

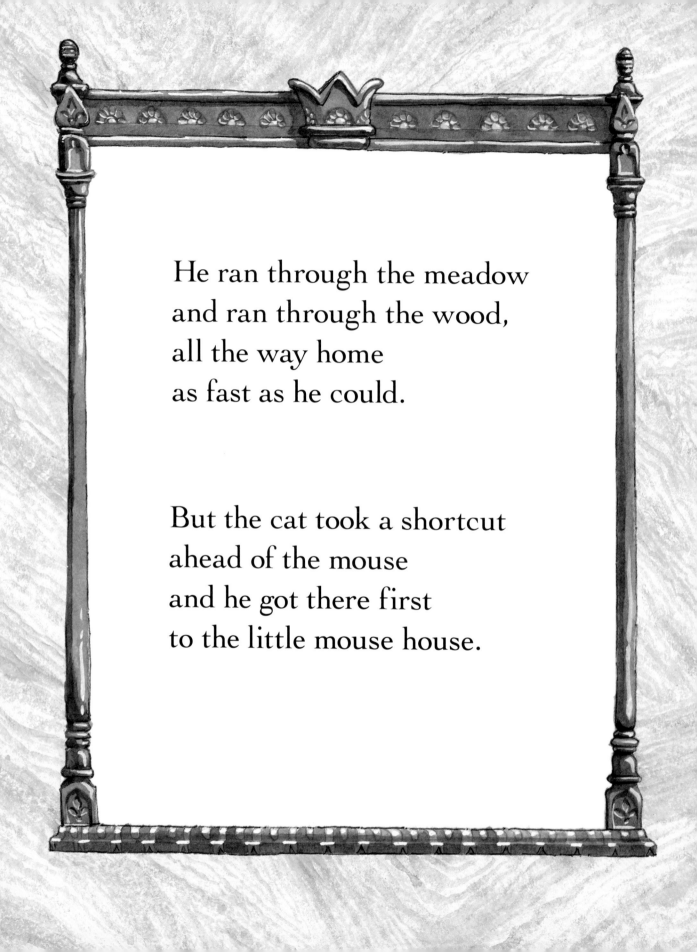

He ran through the meadow
and ran through the wood,
all the way home
as fast as he could.

But the cat took a shortcut
ahead of the mouse
and he got there first
to the little mouse house.

His eyes were a-twinkle,
his face was a-grin,
and he opened his mouth
to welcome Mouse in.

The little mouse knew
he had lost the race.
There was nowhere to go,
there was no hiding place.

But he didn't lose hope,
and quick as a wink,
that frightened little mouse
started to think.

"O beautiful cat,
you wondrous thing,
a meal of one mouse
is not fit for a king.
You should be dining
on silver sardines . . .
and slices of tuna
with long green beans.

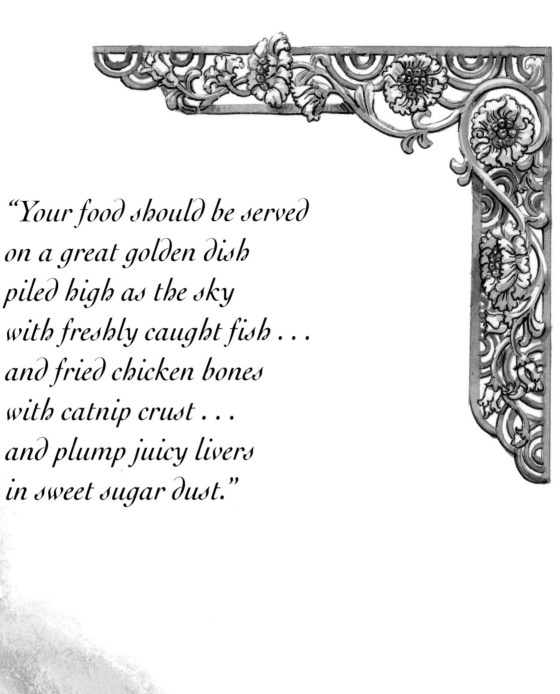

"Your food should be served
on a great golden dish
piled high as the sky
with freshly caught fish . . .
and fried chicken bones
with catnip crust . . .
and plump juicy livers
in sweet sugar dust."

The cat closed his eyes.
He couldn't resist
thinking, *"Yes, it is true!*
I'm a big king cat.
I am worthy of this!*"*

And at that very moment
the smart little mouse
slipped under the cat
and into his house.

"Mother, O mother,
I learned today
that teasing the cat
is dangerous play."

And waving good-bye
to the big fat cat,
he slammed the door!
And that was that!